Partners in Crime

by

Nigel Hinton

First published in 2003 in Great Britain by
Barrington Stoke Ltd
18 Walker St, Edinburgh, EH3 7LP

www.barringtonstoke.co.uk

Reprinted 2004, 2005, 2006, 2007

ISBN: 978-1-84299-102-2

Printed in Great Britain by Bell & Bain Ltd

A Note from the Author

This story started when I was listening to an old song about a man who finds his wife in bed with another man. It was a violent and dramatic song and I couldn't get it out of my head. I tried to imagine the pain and hatred that could send someone mad enough to go out and kill.

Suddenly I had this idea about some boys who meet at primary school. I thought about the complicated things that can go on between friends – the needing, the jealousy, the power struggles, the love and the heartbreak. I imagined the boys growing up, caught up together in a tough, dirty world but having fun, making money, meeting girls. And then, I thought: supposing there's this special girl ...

To Wes Stace and Alan Tunbridge –
with thanks for all the help and
encouragement

Contents

Chapter 1
The Truth

DRUG GANG KILLINGS was the headline news in the *Evening Star*.

The TV and newspaper reporters, the police, the public – everybody believed that the deaths were caused by a war between drug dealers.

They all got it wrong.

Only one person knows the truth. Me – Perry Grant.

The deaths weren't anything to do with drugs. Like the song says, 'Love is the Answer'. Blood was spilled and people died, because of love. Love and revenge.

Chapter 2

You're Dead Meat!

'Love is the Answer' was the Number One song the year Toddie, Marco and I all met up. We were ten years old.

Toddie was King of Year 5 at Heeton Junior School. Of course he was King. Toddie was King wherever he was.

Marco and I were the new boys at school. I moved there because my mum decided to leave my dad and go back to the town where she was born. I went with her.

I knew she didn't really want me. "They ruin your life, kids," she told everyone. But even she couldn't leave me with my dad. He was a mean pig who drank too much and knocked me and my mum about.

It was strange – I hated living in the same house as my dad but when we moved away I started to miss him. I dreamed about him a lot and I always woke up feeling sad. I still do, sometimes.

Marco was at Heeton Junior because it was the nearest school to Stone House – a Home run by Social Services.

Marco's mum and dad were Italian. They came to England and opened an Italian restaurant. One summer they left Marco with his aunt and went back to Italy for a holiday. Their plane crashed in the Alps and they were killed.

Marco was eight at the time. He lived with his aunt in Leeds for a while but she had kids of her own and when he was ten, she decided she couldn't look after him any more. She asked Social Services for help and Marco was placed in Stone House.

Marco was a small, quiet boy who almost never spoke in class. And during break-time he always stood by himself at the edge of the playground, not joining in the games.

Then, one day towards the end of the first term, a Year 6 bully called James Cole picked on Marco. It was all about nothing. Marco just happened to bump into him in the corridor. Cole pushed Marco against the wall and punched him in the guts. Marco fell to the ground and Cole kicked him.

Marco tried to get up and Cole kicked him again. Hard. This time, Marco didn't get up. He lay there groaning, with tears running down his face.

Then Toddie stepped forward. He got hold of Cole and twisted his arm behind his back. He spoke quietly but I was close enough to hear what he said.

"You touch him again – now or ever – and you're dead meat," Toddie hissed. "Get it?"

James Cole was big and strong but Toddie was bigger and stronger. Even the kids from Year 6 knew that Toddie was King of Year 5 and they were scared of him.

"Get it?" Toddie asked again, jerking Cole's arm.

"Yeah, yeah – OK!" Cole squealed.

Toddie jerked Cole's arm once more then let him go. Cole went running off down the corridor.

Toddie helped Marco to his feet.

Again, I was close enough to hear what Toddie whispered, "Don't let 'em see you crying."

Marco nodded and quickly wiped his eyes.

Toddie walked off towards our classroom and we all followed.

From that day onwards, Toddie was Marco's hero. Marco didn't make it obvious but I noticed. I make it my business to notice things. You never know when it might come in useful.

I knew how Marco felt because Toddie was my hero, too. He was big and strong, the opposite of me. He scared me but I was drawn to him. I wanted to be like him.

Chapter 3

The After Hours Crew

At the end of Year 6 most kids in our class chose to go on to James Lint College but Toddie decided to go to Cranston High School. So, of course, Marco and I went there, too.

In the first term at Cranston, Toddie had three big fights with older boys. He won them all and quickly became King of the Lower School. All the other tough kids flocked to his side.

Marco and I weren't very tough so Toddie paid no attention to us until we got the exam results at the end of the year. Marco got top marks in every subject except Maths and Art – I was the one who got the top marks in those.

On the last day before the summer holidays I saw Toddie walk over to Marco in the playground so I moved near enough to hear what he said.

"Hey, genius!" Toddie laughed. "How do you do it? Top in everything!"

Marco blushed and grinned.

"What about me?" I wanted to shout. "I was top in Maths and Art – not him." But I kept quiet.

"I might need a bit of help next year," Toddie went on. "You know, a quick look at your homework before I do mine – that kind of stuff. OK?"

Marco acted cool – thought about it a long time as if he couldn't make up his mind – then he nodded, "Yeah, OK."

The next term all the teachers were amazed by the improvement in Toddie's work. Until one day Mr Forbes realised what was happening.

"That's strange, Todd," Mr Forbes said, holding up Toddie's homework. "Your answers are exactly the same as Marco's. Now how did that happen?"

"Dunno," Toddie mumbled.

"Well, I do know. You cheated."

"No, Sir."

"Don't lie to me, Todd. Go and see the Head."

"It wasn't Toddie," Marco said. "It was me. I asked him if I could copy his work."

Mr Forbes knew that wasn't true but there was nothing he could do. Marco stuck to his story and he was the one who was punished.

"You're my man!" Toddie said, putting his arm round Marco's shoulder after the lesson. "I owe you."

"No problem," Marco said.

"Except I'll start getting crap grades again," Toddie grumbled.

"Not if you stop being a lazy git!" Marco said.

Toddie laughed. Only Marco could say something like that to him and get away with it.

"Listen," Marco went on, "why don't we work together after school? I could explain stuff to you and you wouldn't need to copy from me."

Toddie looked surprised at the idea but after a moment he nodded, "Yeah, why not?"

So, every evening after school Marco and Toddie went to the library and worked for an hour. Marco called it *The After Hours Crew*. I burned with jealousy and I kept asking to join.

"I can help you with Maths," I said to them one day. "Oh, go on – please, Dad."

They burst out laughing. I felt like an idiot but my silly mistake won them round. They finally said yes and I started to work with them.

The funny thing was, Toddie didn't just get better marks, he enjoyed the work, too. One day a boy saw us working in the library and called us boffins but Toddie just stood up and smacked him in the mouth. Nobody called us boffins again.

Toddie was King of the school and we were the Princes. Well, Marco was the Prince. I was the faithful dog who ran after both of them. I knew the truth – Toddie and Marco were the real mates. They just put up with me. But I knew that one day my time would come.

Chapter 4

Mystery Money

"Why didn't you tell us?" Toddie said when he found out it was Marco's fifteenth birthday.

"I forgot."

"How can you forget your own birthday?" Toddie asked.

"Well, they don't make much fuss about birthdays at Stone House," Marco explained.

"Yeah, but we could have sent you a card or something – couldn't we, Perry?" Toddie said.

I nodded.

"It's not every day you're 15," Toddie went on. "Come on. We've got to celebrate."

"What about our work?" Marco said.

"Stuff the work for tonight," Toddie said. "We're going to celebrate. I'm buying."

We went to Burger King and Toddie paid for our meals. Then he bought some cans of lager and we went to the park to drink them.

"Why are you still at Stone House, Marco?" Toddie asked as we sat on the old bandstand and watched some young kids playing football. "I mean, don't they try and get you adopted or fostered or something?"

"Yeah – but I keep saying no."

"Why?" Toddie asked.

"Well, just 'cos my mum and dad are dead, it doesn't mean I want some strangers to take over my life."

"It's got to be better than being in a Home," Toddie said.

"No!" Marco said fiercely and I saw his eyes start to water. "I love my mum and dad and nobody's going to take their place – never."

"I know what Marco means," I said. "My mum's got a new boyfriend. I hate his guts and I don't want him acting like he's my dad. No way."

Marco looked at me and smiled and I suddenly felt as if we understood each other. It was almost as if we were real friends.

"Oh well, cheers," Toddie said clinking his can against ours. "Happy Birthday, mate. Tell you what, when I get my own place you can leave that Stone dump and live with me. We'll pull all the chicks and have a right laugh."

I don't think Marco believed that Toddie would be able to pay for his own place for years, but I did. I'd noticed something – Toddie always had loads of cash. In fact, when he took out his wallet to pay for the burgers, I'd seen a thick wad of money. Toddie's family wasn't rich. He had five brothers and sisters and his mum's job didn't pay very well. So where was the money coming from?

I made up my mind to find out.

Chapter 5
Toddie's Secret

It didn't take me long to find out why Toddie had so much money. All I had to do was keep a close eye on him.

On Friday evening he left his house at about nine o' clock and I followed him. He went into a block of flats and I hid in the shadows, waiting. Twenty minutes later he came out. He checked up and down the street before he set off again, heading for the centre of town.

For the next three hours he stood in an alley next to a club called *Seventh Heaven*.

I watched from a dark doorway across the road. It was the most popular club in town and a lot of the clubbers paid a little visit to Toddie before they went in. The light from the club's neon sign spilled down the alley and I could see Toddie and his customers lit up by the flashes of red, blue and green. The people handed money to him and he gave them little packets in return. It didn't take a genius to guess what was in the packets.

So, I had found out Toddie's secret and I knew it could be useful to me.

All week I thought hard and finally came up with a plan. First of all I checked the alley next to *Seventh Heaven*. There was a fence at the far end but it would be easy to climb into the park on the other side. Good – there was an escape route.

The next Friday evening I followed Toddie again, from his house to the block of flats, and then from the block of flats to the alley outside *Seventh Heaven.* As soon as he started to serve his first customers, I ran to the nearest phone box and rang the police.

"Hello," I said. "There's a fight going on in the alley next to *Seventh Heaven.* I think someone's hurt – there's blood everywhere. You'd better come quick!"

I slammed the phone down before they had a chance to ask questions. Then I ran back to the alley. Toddie was just handing a packet over to a customer.

"Hiya, Toddie!" I said.

The neon light flashed green on Toddie's scared face as he spun round to me.

"Perry!" he said, hiding the packet behind his back. "What are you doing here?"

"I was just going past and I saw you. What are you up to?"

"Oh, nothing much," Toddie lied. "Might go clubbing."

"Hey, you – what about my tabs?" the customer said. "Come on, where are they?"

Toddie had no choice – he pulled his hand from behind his back and handed over the packet. The customer walked away.

"Toddie, are you ...?" I said, looking at him all wide-eyed and innocent. "Are you selling ...?"

"Push off, Perry! Forget you ever saw me here, right?" Toddie warned. "Push off, I said!"

I turned and started to walk away – then I stopped, as if I'd just remembered something.

"Toddie, listen," I said, hurrying back. "I was going past the Manhattan Club a couple of minutes ago and I saw the cops arresting someone. Maybe they're doing raids tonight."

Toddie was still taking this in when a couple of customers came down the alley towards us.

"I'll keep a look-out while you sort these two, OK?" I said quickly.

Toddie nodded.

I ran to the end of the alley and looked along the road. No police car yet. I prayed that it would come soon.

Toddie had just finished serving the two customers when I saw a flashing blue light at the end of the road. The police were coming.

"It's them!" I shouted.

Toddie started to run towards me.

"Not that way – it's too late," I said, grabbing him and pulling him back down the alley.

As we got to the fence, the police jumped out of the car and started down the alley after us. We climbed the fence, dropped down the other side, and raced across the park. When we looked back, there was no sign of the cops – they had given up the chase.

"Thanks, Perry," Toddie said, leaning against a tree to get his breath back.

"No problem."

"No, I mean it. I owe you."

"That's what friends are for," I said.

Toddie smiled and nodded.

I grinned. I was in with Toddie. And I was going to keep it that way.

Chapter 6

Four Hooded Men

From then on, I helped Toddie on Friday and Saturday evenings. At first I just kept a look-out for the cops but soon I was taking care of all the money.

Toddie couldn't hide it at his place with all his brothers and sisters around, so I looked after it. My mum was out with her boyfriend most of the time and anyway she never went near my room so I could keep it safe. I locked the money in a box and hid it under the floorboards. And I kept perfect accounts of how much money we made and how much we paid out. My maths was coming in useful.

"You haven't told Marco about all this, have you?" Toddie asked one day.

"Why? Don't you trust him?"

"Don't be stupid – he's my best friend. Of course I trust him, it's just that ... Well, he's not like you and me. He's got class."

"He's an orphan, Toddie! He lives in a crappy children's home – what kind of class is that?"

"Yeah, but ... there's just something about him. You know those fairy stories where some poor kid turns out to be a prince or something? Well, he's like that."

"Oh yeah, Prince Marco," I sneered.

Toddie gave me an angry look.

"No, I know what you mean," I said quickly. "He's something special."

Actually, there really was something special about Marco, even I had to admit. He had become very good-looking with his dark eyes and his dark curls and sexy smile, and all the girls fancied him like mad. But it was more than that – he was cool. He kind of lived in his own world. He didn't worry about trying to fit in or trying to make people like him. Toddie was right – Marco had class.

"Well, anyway," Toddie said, "I don't want him to know about all this."

So we didn't tell Marco. But we kept on dealing drugs and the money rolled in. Soon there were five full boxes under my floorboards.

"Listen, Toddie – we're going to have to put it in the bank," I said one day.

"You're mad – people'll want to know where it comes from."

"Not if we put it in a lot of different bank accounts. Look, leave it to me. I'll fix it – I promise."

I did fix it. I asked people and I read a lot, and I found out the best way of hiding money in different accounts. Toddie was impressed. He was even more impressed with my next idea.

"I've been thinking," I said one evening when we were outside *Seventh Heaven*. "That guy you buy the stuff from – the one who lives in the flats."

"Leroy? What about him?"

"Where does he get the stuff from?"

"From some guys in Essex," Toddie said.

"What would happen if we cut out Leroy and went straight to the guys in Essex?"

"Leroy wouldn't be happy."

"Do we care?" I asked.

Toddie thought about this then he laughed. "You cunning little devil," he said, putting his arms around my shoulders. I felt great.

Three weeks later we started getting our stuff direct from the guys from Essex. Leroy wasn't happy.

One night he burst into Toddie's house. Toddie's mum was out but his young brothers and sisters were there. They ran into a bedroom and hid while Leroy shouted at Toddie, threatening to kill him. He smashed the TV and a couple of windows before Toddie managed to shove him out of the door.

The next day Leroy came out of his flat and found four hooded men waiting for him. He tried to run but the men caught him and broke both his legs.

Toddie sent him a Get Well Soon card in hospital.

Chapter 7
That Crazy Look

At the end of Year 11, Toddie and I left school but Marco stayed on to do more exams. We still saw him a lot, of course, and every couple of months Toddie took him shopping for new clothes.

"They don't dress you right at that Stone place. I don't want my mate going round looking like a loser," Toddie said.

"Yeah, but I can't keep taking your money," Marco said.

"Listen – all we've got is each other. Your parents are dead. Perry's mum doesn't give a toss about him. And my old lady only cares about where the next bottle of booze is coming from. We're family, you and me and Perry. We can trust each other. So it's one for all, and all for one – right? Right?"

"Right," Marco said. "But where does all the money come from?"

"I told you – Perry and me are buying and selling."

"Buying and selling what?"

"Oh, computer parts, antiques, all sorts. We're doing great. Come on, let's do a bit of shopping and go down the pub."

During the next year, Toddie and I built up our business. We did well. Toddie did *very* well – he took 80 per cent of the profits. It wasn't fair but I didn't bother to argue. I still got better money than I could get anywhere else.

In fact we were making so much money that by the time he was 17 Toddie had enough to buy a house. It was me who organised it all. It wasn't a big house and it wasn't in the best part of town, but it was his own place.

As promised, the first thing Toddie did was to invite Marco to live there. "You're 17 – you can leave that Stone dump and move in with me tomorrow," he said.

"Thanks, Toddie, but not yet," Marco said.

"Why not? We'll have a laugh!"

"I know but I'd never get any work done. I really want to get my A Levels."

"OK," Toddie said, looking disappointed. "But the minute the exams are over, you're moving in here – right?"

"OK."

"Promise?"

"Promise," Marco laughed.

"I could move in with you, Toddie," I said.

"I don't think so, Perry. This place is too small. Maybe when I get somewhere bigger."

"Yes, but if there's room for Marco ..."
I began then stopped as I saw the crazy look in Toddie's eyes.

I knew that look. That crazy look. It meant – don't argue. It meant – don't say another word. I'd seen that look so many times. And a couple of times I'd seen what happened to people who ignored it. I'd seen Toddie beat them until they begged for mercy.

"OK?" he asked, that crazy look beginning to fade. I smiled and nodded, but inside I hurt like hell.

"One day," I thought. "One day you'll be sorry."

Chapter 8
Big Money

We were going up in the world.

We stopped standing in the cold and rain outside clubs and we hired some young guys to sell the drugs for us. One of the new guys tried to cheat us but my accounts soon showed what he was up to.

Toddie paid him a visit. When the guy was able to talk again he told people what Toddie had done to him and no-one ever tried to cheat us again.

I started reading the money pages in the newspapers and, without telling Toddie, I took some money out of the bank accounts and invested it in shares. He was angry when I told him what I'd done but he calmed down when I showed him the profit we'd made. "Is that right?" he said. "The money's doubled in three months?"

"You know what they say – it's not bank robbers who earn the big money, it's the people who own the banks. Why don't we set up an investment company? A legal business where we can hide the drugs money."

Toddie thought about it for a few days, then he agreed, "It's a great idea. Marco can run it – he'll need a job when he finishes school."

"But it's my idea," I said. "Marco doesn't know anything about money."

"He can learn," said Toddie. "Anyway, you can do the real work behind the scenes. He'll just be the front man who meets the customers. You know what a charmer he is. People will fall over themselves to give him their money."

I was glad Marco didn't seem at all keen on the idea.

"I want to go on with my studies," he told Toddie. "Maybe go to university."

"University? You can't!" Toddie said. "You said you were going to move in with me."

"I know but all the teachers reckon that ..."

"Teachers! What do they know?" Toddie sneered. "You could go to stupid university and end up broke. Plenty of students do."

"I know, but ..."

"You promised! You said you'd leave Stone House and come and live with me."

Toddie was starting to get angry. I saw that look come into his eye. But Marco was the only person who wasn't scared by that look. He put his hand gently on Toddie's shoulder and the crazy look faded away.

"Oh come on, Marco – we're family," Toddie said, almost begging now. "It'll be great. We can call it Marco Investments. Your own business at 18 – just think how proud your mum and dad would have been."

He was clever, was Toddie. He'd mentioned the one thing that Marco couldn't resist – his parents.

"Yeah, OK," Marco said.

A huge smile of relief spread across Toddie's face and I almost felt sorry for him.

He loved Marco. I don't mean he was gay and fancied him, I mean he really loved him as a friend. And Marco felt the same way about him. It's rare, that kind of love, and I knew they didn't feel like that about me.

So we set up our own company, Marco Investments. Toddie was right – the customers were charmed by Marco and money poured in. I did all the real work, watching the money markets and making the investments. I was good at it and we started to make big profits. And behind it all, the drugs were making us even more money.

The next two years were fantastic. Toddie bought a bigger and better house and Marco moved in with him. I bought a small flat a couple of streets away.

We were the richest and coolest young guys in town. We all got flash cars and the latest designer clothes. And every weekend, Toddie and Marco had non-stop parties at their place – the best booze, the best drugs and the best girls.

It's funny what money can do. I'm not a good-looking guy – in fact, like my mother always says, I'm short and ugly – but some girls will do anything for you as long as you've got money. Oh, the girls at those parties didn't fall in love with me the way they did with Toddie and Marco, but I still got plenty of what I wanted.

Yes, they were great years.

Then Lady came into our lives.

Chapter 9
Lady

The first time I saw Nadia she was naked.

I used to go to Art class every Tuesday evening at the local college. I never told the others, of course – I knew they would just laugh. But I was good at drawing and I loved the classes. Our Art teacher used to bring in all kinds of things for us to draw – bits of cars, old bottles, bones, anything. One evening, we had a nude model – it was Nadia.

She came into the room, took off her dressing gown, and sat on a chair facing the

41

class. She was so beautiful. I tried to draw her but my hands were shaking.

I made a bad sketch of her body then I tried to draw her face. I saw the way her chin was raised, brave and proud, as if she was saying – 'I'm naked but I don't care'. But then I looked at her eyes and I saw that she was scared. Scared and hurt.

I tried to go on drawing but I kept looking back at her eyes. And I felt as if I knew her. I felt as if we were alike. And I began to hate all the people in the room. I didn't want them looking at this young girl sitting there naked and so scared.

I left the class early and went down to the canteen. I was still there half an hour later when Nadia came in. Her clothes were old and too big for her and she looked even younger than before. She bought a cup of tea and then looked round for somewhere to sit. All the other tables were full. She walked up to my table and pointed at the empty chair opposite me.

"I can?" she said in a strong foreign accent.

I nodded.

She sat down and looked straight into my eyes. "You are there – for drawing. I see you," she said. "Why you leave?"

"I ... I ... felt sorry for you."

"Sorry?"

"Yeah. I mean, how old are you?" I asked.

"Nineteen."

"That's younger than me. You're young, you're beautiful. You shouldn't be doing stuff like ..."

There was a flash of anger in her eyes. For a moment I thought she was going to get up and leave but then she took a sip of tea.

"I need money," she said. The word came out as *morney*. "I not do bad thing."

"No," I said, "but ..."

"I come from Russia. My mother and sister also. We want to stay here. My mother is sick. My sister is little. I must find job. Is hard. So, I find this."

She took another sip of tea and I saw her looking at the bag of crisps on the table.

"Are you hungry?" I asked.

She nodded.

I gave her the crisps then went over to the counter and bought her a burger and chips and beans. She ate it fast and scraped the plate clean.

"Thank you," she said when she finished. She reached across the table and put her hand on top of mine. "You are nice man."

She took her hand away and I wanted her to touch me again.

"Would you like a proper meal? Tomorrow?" I asked. "We could go to a restaurant."

She said yes.

We met the next day. And the day after that. And the day after that.

I was in love. Crazy, stupid, head over heels in love. And you know what they say – love is blind. I was blind. All I could see was Nadia. Her tumbling, black hair. Those clear, green eyes. That open smile. My Lady. That's what I called her – Lady.

Lady moved into my flat.

"What about your mother and sister?" I asked her, the day she moved in.

Lady looked away.

"Where are they living? Do they know you're here?"

Lady kept her eyes down. And I knew – there wasn't a mother or a sister. She had been lying to me. And every time she talked about her life in Russia the stories changed. Sometimes she told me she had grown up in a city with her mother and father, sometimes she said she had grown up in a small village with her grandmother.

I didn't care about the lies. She had lived through bad times – perhaps she lied in order to survive. I loved her and that was all I cared about. She wasn't like those girls at the parties who only went with me for my money. Lady wanted me, needed me.

For three months it was just the two of us. We hardly went anywhere. I loved coming home, knowing that she would be there. I loved cooking meals for her. I loved watching TV with her by my side. I loved holding her in the night. And I loved waking up next to her in the morning.

Then, like an idiot, I let her meet Toddie.

Chapter 10
A Stupid Mistake

It was my own fault – I wanted to show off Lady. I wanted Toddie and the others to see that I had a beautiful girlfriend. I took her to one of his famous parties.

Marco wasn't there that evening – he was away for the weekend. But Toddie was there and you should have seen his face when I walked in with Lady.

"Hello, darling," Toddie said, pulling her towards him as he shook her hand. "What's your name?"

"Nadia. But Perry call me Lady," she laughed, a bit embarrassed when he wouldn't let go of her hand.

"Does he? Romantic little runt, isn't he!" Toddie said. "Well, enjoy the party. I'll catch you later."

Lady and I started to walk away but he pulled me back.

"You sneaky little git! Where did you find her?" he whispered. "Great legs. And what a bum!"

I shook his hand off my arm and he laughed at my anger, "Just kidding, mate!"

The house was packed with people and I managed to keep Lady away from Toddie all evening. At midnight I decided to leave, hoping to get out of the house without seeing him, but he caught us at the front door.

"Going already?" he said, grabbing Lady's hand. "We haven't had a chance to talk. Still, there'll be plenty of time to get to know each other."

He winked at her then kissed her hand. I saw his teeth nip her skin. She blushed and looked at me.

"Lay off it, Toddie!" I said.

"Just being polite," he laughed.

I pulled Lady's hand away from him and for a moment that crazy look came into his eyes. Then he laughed again and opened the door to let us out.

"See you soon," he called as we walked down the path.

I knew I should never have brought her. I'd made a stupid mistake.

Chapter 11
Share and Share Alike

The next day Toddie came round to my flat. I was sure he'd only come to see Lady but when we went into the living room he flicked his fingers at her.

"Here you, turn that telly off and get lost. I want to talk to Perry – in private," he ordered.

Lady looked at me. I nodded and she left the room.

"I've had this idea," Toddie said when we were alone. "I need your advice."

I was flattered and I listened carefully while he told me his plan to take over the drug trade in nearby Morford.

"The Kelly brothers run the drugs business in Morford. Won't there be trouble?" I said.

"Probably. But I've got the backing of the big boys in Essex."

"Yeah, but if the Kellys turn nasty ..."

"Then I'll have to turn even nastier, won't I?" Toddie laughed.

The next evening he came to my flat again. Again he sent Lady out of the room and again he talked about his plans to get rid of the Kellys. But this time he stayed longer and, after a while, he called Lady back into the room. "Sorry to keep getting rid of you, love," he said, smiling. "But it's business talk and we don't want to bore you. Come and sit down next to me – I won't bite, I promise."

Lady sat down on the sofa near him.

"Cor, you've made this place look nice," he said. "It was a right toilet when Perry was on his own. He's a slob – don't know how you put up with him."

I sat there, helpless, while he joked and laughed with Lady for nearly an hour.

"Toddie, please don't," I whispered to him at the front door as he was leaving.

"Don't what?" he asked.

"You know. Lady's mine."

"We're friends – share and share alike," he grinned.

"No, please," I said.

"Don't worry – I'm only kidding," he said, punching my arm.

But he was back the next evening. And the evening after that. And the evening after that. He hadn't wanted my advice. It had just been an excuse and now he didn't even bother making up excuses.

Lady started off being cold towards him. "He is cruel man," she said to me after his first visit. "He push you around."

"He's my friend."

"I do not like him," she said.

But night after night I saw her beginning to give in to his bullying ways. What could I do? He was big and tough and powerful and I wasn't. One evening I was standing next to Toddie and I saw Lady looking at us. And I suddenly saw myself through her eyes – so small and weak and ugly compared to him.

She meant everything to me. And I wanted to mean everything to her. Stupid idiot! How could a beautiful girl like Lady ever love someone like me? It was breaking my heart.

Then the trouble with the Kellys started and we didn't have time for anything else.

Chapter 12
It's War

The Kellys beat up one of our dealers in Morford. They left him, tied up, outside Toddie's house with a note pinned to his bloody shirt. The note read, 'Keep out of Morford'.

A week later, another of our Morford dealers was thrown out of a car onto the road outside Toddie's house. He was alive – but only just.

Toddie hired two more dealers and sent them to Morford. They were both beaten up.

"Right then – it's war," Toddie said.

The next evening he came round to my flat again. He snapped his fingers at Lady and sent her out of the room. I could see she was upset but she left.

"OK, now listen," Toddie said. "I'm off to Spain for a few months."

"Why?"

"I'm going to get some people to sort out the Kellys and I don't want to be around when it happens, do I? That way no-one can blame me, can they? You just lie low and make sure Marco doesn't find out what's going on. I'm trusting you."

The next day Toddie flew to Spain.
Lady cried when she heard that he had gone.

Three weeks later the two Kelly brothers were found dead in their car. Someone had driven them to a lonely lane outside Morford and shot them through the head. Toddie had got his revenge.

As soon as Toddie had left for Spain, I did everything I could to win back Lady's love. I bought her flowers and presents and took her out to the best restaurants.

One weekend I took her to London. We stayed in a top hotel and we went shopping in all the best designer shops.

"You are a good man, Perry. You buy me so many things," she said as we lay in bed that night.

"I want to show you how much I love you," I whispered.

"You can. You can show me. You buy me a passport."

"A passport?"

"Yes. I want more than anything. Is possible?" she asked.

"Sure – anything's possible. But why?"

"I am illegal – they can send me back. I want to be English. Bad, bad things happen to me in Russia. I want to stay here with you. You make me feel safe, Perry. You make me happy."

I held her tight so that she couldn't see my tears of happiness. And I promised I would get her a passport – the best fake passport that money could buy.

I rang my contacts and a couple of weeks later the passport arrived.

"See the name on it?" I said, showing it to her. "Mrs Nadia Grant. It's like we're married."

"So, now I am English," she said. "No—one can make me go back to Russia. I have passport. I can go anywhere?"

"Anywhere in the world."

Three weeks later I got back from work and the flat was empty. Her clothes had gone from the cupboard. Her make-up and things had gone from the bathroom. There was a big note lying on the bed. It just had one word on it – 'Sorry'. One word and three kisses. The last kiss was smeared, as if she'd been crying when she'd written it.

I rang the local taxi company and found out that she had gone to the airport. I rang all the airlines and found out what I had already guessed – a passenger called Mrs Nadia Grant had taken the evening flight to Spain.

Chapter 13
The Really Dirty Stuff

Every week Toddie called me from Spain. I only mentioned Lady once. I needed to know that she was safe. "Is she there, Toddie? Is she OK?"

"Of course she's OK – she's with me. The best man won. No hard feelings, eh?"

We never talked about her again. When he called he chatted about the weather and I gave him the news about the business. One week I told him the police had just paid a visit to Marco Investments. "They were asking questions about you and the Kellys," I told him.

"What did you say?"

"That I'd never heard of the Kelly brothers. And that you'd been in Spain for the last three months."

"Good. Do you think they'll be back?"

"No – they've got nothing to go on, and they know it."

What I didn't tell him was that Marco had been really shaken up by the police visit.

Poor Marco, he was so honest and innocent. Toddie was still his hero and Toddie could do no wrong. Marco knew we were involved in drugs, of course – it had been impossible to hide that. But Toddie had lied and said that it was only cannabis.

"You know me, Marco," Toddie had said. "I wouldn't sell hard drugs."

So Marco had no idea about the really dirty stuff we were involved in – the junkies, the threats, the bribes, the beatings-up, the overdoses, the deaths.

I was so hurt and angry about Lady that I nearly told him what Toddie was really like. Nearly told him what his hero had done to the Kellys. Nearly told him where the money for Marco Investments came from.

But I knew what would happen if I did – Marco would walk out. And Toddie would never forgive me. So I kept quiet. It was strange – part of me hated Toddie but part of me still needed him, still longed to be his friend.

Then one evening Marco came round to my flat. I drank too much and started talking about Lady. I missed her terribly and all the pain in my heart came pouring out. Suddenly I broke down and cried.

"Listen, mate," Marco said, trying to cheer me up. "Why not come and stay at my place while Toddie's away? You're gonna go mad, stuck here on your own."

I accepted his offer. I stayed with him for over two months and we got on really well. We talked about everything. I told him things about myself that I'd never told anyone. Things about Lady, things about how my mum treated me. I even told him how I dreamed about my dad.

And Marco told me things about himself – about how he wanted to visit the site of his parents' plane crash and how one day he would like to take time off from Marco Investments and go to university. We chatted and laughed and shared secrets like real friends and I felt closer to him than ever.

Then Toddie came back from Spain with Lady.

I moved back to my lonely flat. Night after night I sat there alone thinking about Toddie. It wasn't fair. He had everything – my girlfriend and my best friend.

But not for long.

Chapter 14
He'll Kill Me!

Toddie never said he was sorry about Lady – not once. He even joked about it the first time I saw them together after they got back.

"Perry, this is Lady ... Oops, I forgot – you two know each other, don't you!"

Lady blushed and kept looking at the floor. She seemed thin and pale, not like someone who'd just come back from sunny Spain.

As I was leaving, Lady finally looked at me. It was only a quick glance but there was a sadness in her eyes. My heart jumped and I wondered if that sad look was because she missed me.

"Don't, Perry," I told myself. "Don't get yourself hurt again. You've got over her. Forget her."

But I was lying to myself. I hadn't got over her. I couldn't forget her.

I kept hoping she would phone me or write to me. I knew I was being stupid but I couldn't stop thinking, *Maybe she'll come back to me. Maybe she'll come back.*

Months and months passed. I kept on working with Toddie and I never let on how I felt.

I talked and laughed. I lived my life and never let him see what I was feeling.

Bit by bit, my hopes began to fade. Then one evening there was a knock at my door and Lady was standing there. She looked scared and ill.

"Don't tell Toddie I come here," she begged.

"OK," I said.

As soon as she sat down on the sofa, tears filled her eyes. I sat next to her and held her tight while she cried.

"Oh Perry ... Why? Why I leave you?" she said between sobs. "I am an idiot. Kill me, kill me. I am an idiot."

"Ssh, it's OK, it's OK," I said. "You can come back."

"No, I can't," she sobbed. "Toddie will take me away. And ... I need him."

She turned her arm over and I saw the needle marks and the bruises.

Toddie had done this to her. I'd seen it happen before, to other girls. Sometimes I wondered if it was his way of making sure girls stayed with him – get them hooked on drugs. But how could he have done it to Lady? To my Lady?

A huge rush of anger and hatred filled my heart. I would get him. I would make him pay for this.

"What are you doing – smack?" I asked.

She nodded.

"How long?"

"Since I go to Spain."

"You can get off it."

"No. I need it, Perry," she said.

"You can get off it, I promise. I'll help you. We'll get you into a rehab clinic."

"Toddie will not let me go – I know this," she said.

"He won't be able to stop you. Give me a couple of days. Go back to him and pretend everything's OK. I'll fix things, make plans. I'll get you away from him and off the drugs, I promise."

I held onto Lady until she stopped crying. Then I drove her back to Toddie's house.

I stopped at the end of the road so nobody would see us. "It's going to be OK," I said, grabbing her hand as she got out of the car. "I promise."

She nodded. I kissed her fingers then let her go.

I drove back to my flat and started making my plans.

Chapter 15
Pay-back Time

I was patient. I made myself wait.

All I wanted to do was to take Lady away, far away where Toddie could never touch her again. But I had to be clever and wait for the right moment.

Finally, the moment came. Toddie went to London for a big meeting with the guys from Essex. That morning I sat in my car near his house. I watched as he drove away, then I waited until Marco left to go to work.

"Pack your stuff," I told Lady when I ran into the house.

"Why? Where we go?"

"We're leaving this place – forever. I've booked you into a clinic."

"Perry, I don't know ... if Toddie finds me..."

"He won't," I said. "Now hurry."

We packed quickly and put her bags in the car.

"I must check I not leave anything," Lady said.

She went back into the house and I waited in the car, praying that Toddie or Marco wouldn't come back suddenly.

The minutes ticked by and I got more and more nervous. "Come on, Lady, hurry up," I called as I went back into the house.

I found her in the bathroom. She was on her knees, leaning over the bath with a needle in her hand.

"No, no Perry. Please," she said as I snatched the needle away from her. "Only one hit! The last. Please!"

"No! It's over. You're stopping now," I shouted.

The clinic was 80 miles away and she cried the whole journey. Then, when we got to the clinic, she begged me not to leave her. It broke my heart to see her like that but I couldn't let her tears change my mind.

"I'll come and see you as often as I can," I promised. "You've got to be strong. I love you, Lady."

Late that evening I got a phone call from Toddie. He had just got back from London.

"Perry, do you know where Lady is?"

"No, why?"

"She's not here. All her stuff's gone. Where the hell is she?"

I could hear the pain and worry in his voice and I wanted to laugh. At last! It was pay-back time. Now he knew what it felt like.

"Maybe she's gone off with someone," I said, rubbing it in. "You know what she's like."

The next day Toddie came into the office at Marco Investments. There were dark rings round his eyes and it was obvious that he hadn't slept.

"I'm really sorry, mate," I said, giving him a hug. "I've called everyone I know – they're all on the look-out. We're gonna find her."

"Do you think so?"

"Yeah, sure – don't worry."

Every day, I told Toddie not to worry. I was playing my part well. Every day I pretended to cheer him up. I was Perry, the good friend, trying to help my mate.

And every evening I drove the 80 miles to the clinic to see Lady. The first few weeks were hell for her. She was pale and she shivered and cried all the time and told me she wanted to die.

Then, slowly, it all started to change. Lady's eyes grew brighter. Her voice was stronger. There was colour in her cheeks. She was filled with hope again. She was getting better.

But while she got better, Toddie was getting worse.

"Why? Why?" he kept asking. "Why did she leave me?"

He hardly ate. He drank and smoked too much. He was taking pills to help him sleep. He was taking pills to wake up.

I knew the pain he was going through. And I was glad. I wanted him to suffer – the way I'd suffered. The way he'd made Lady suffer.

And every day I kept the pain going by telling him, "Don't worry, mate, she'll be back."

Finally, Lady was well enough to leave the clinic.

"A few more days, then you can get out of here," I told her. "I've rented a house for you. It's a place out in the country – quiet, peaceful. You'll love it."

"Will you be there?"

"Not all the time, in case Toddie finds out."

"I'm scared, Perry. I might start again. I can't trust myself on my own."

"You won't be on your own," I said. "I've got it all worked out."

Oh yes, I was so clever. I thought I'd got it all worked out.

But I hadn't.

Chapter 16
He's Evil

"When Lady walked out, I lost everything. Everything," Toddie kept saying to me.

And every time he said it, I thought, *No, not everything. Not yet. But you will.*

Two days before Lady was due to leave the clinic, I told Marco the truth about Toddie. We were alone in the office and Marco was going on about how unhappy Toddie was without Lady.

"I know where she is," I said. "I helped her run away."

"What?" Marco said, looking at me in shock. "Why?"

"Because she hates him and she's scared of him. And because he was feeding her smack."

"That's out of order," Marco said. "It's not Toddie's fault she's doing drugs."

"It is, Marco. You don't get it, do you? She was unhappy in Spain. She wanted to come home. He got her hooked on heroin so she wouldn't leave him."

"That's a lie!" Marco shouted

"You're blind, Marco – you can't see what's right in front of your eyes. You think Toddie is God – well, he's not!"

And I told him. About the drugs. About the murders.

Marco didn't like it. He didn't want to believe it. But I had proof – diaries, bank accounts, letters – and I showed him.

For a long time he sat there, silent. Then he clenched his fists in anger.

"You're wrong – I'm not blind. I knew it all the time, really – deep down. I just wouldn't let myself see it. Oh God, I'm so bloody stupid! What am I going to do, Perry? He's evil! I can't go on working for him ... living with him ..."

And that's when I told him about the house in the country and how I needed someone to look after Lady. I gave him a map and the keys. He went back to his house, packed his things, wrote a note for Toddie, and left.

Toddie showed me the note when he found it. All it said was – 'I know about the Kelly brothers. I know about the drugs. You won't see me again'.

"How did he find out? Who told him?" Toddie yelled at me.

I'd got my lie ready. "I don't know," I said. "The cops, maybe. They've been here a couple of times asking questions. Maybe Marco just put two and two together."

Toddie believed me. "I'll kill him!" he said, wildly. "He can't just go off like that, without talking to me. He can't."

And now it really hit him. He'd lost his girlfriend and he'd lost his best mate. He slumped onto my sofa and held his head in his hands.

I looked down at him and smiled. I had won. Toddie wasn't the King anymore. He was a broken man.

Chapter 17

Top of the World

What a turnaround. I felt great. I'd got everything Toddie wanted – I had Lady and Marco – and he didn't even know it.

On weekdays I lived in town and ran Marco Investments on my own. Then, on Friday evenings, I drove out to the country to spend the weekend with Lady and Marco.

"Where do you push off to every Friday?" Toddie asked me.

"I go and see my dad," I lied quickly.

"Your dad?"

"Yeah – we met up again. We get on really well."

"Hey, listen Perry, I've been thinking. I get a bit lonely at my place now ... What I mean is, do you still fancy coming to live there? We could have a laugh."

Toddie was sure I was going to say yes – I could see it in his eyes. So, I took my time. I made him wait.

Then I hit him with it. "It's really nice of you, mate ... but I don't think so. I like my flat too much."

His face fell and I wanted to laugh. He'd lost his girlfriend and his best friend and now he couldn't even have me!

The weekends in the country with Lady and Marco were the happiest times I've ever known. It was just the three of us, living a simple life. We had barbecues. We went for walks. We listened to music or sat around talking. We were just happy to be together.

Lady was back to her old self, laughing and beautiful, the way she'd been when I'd first met her. And Marco was full of life. He had started reading books again and he'd decided to apply for university.

"It's not as if I'm too old," he said.

"Yes you are," Lady laughed. "You and Perry are old men – 22! I am only 20."

"Twenty-one next month," I said, putting my arm round her. "Nearly an old granny!"

She laughed again and kissed my cheek.

I loved her so much.

A new version of the old song 'Love is the Answer' was in the charts that summer and I bought it for her. We sang it all the time and the words said everything I felt:

Why am I on top of the world?

Love is, love is the answer

All it takes is a boy and a girl

Love is, love is the answer.

Why was I on top of the world? Lady was the answer.

Lady's twenty-first birthday was on a Thursday. I rang to wish her happy birthday.

"Hi," she said. "Marco's just opening a bottle of champagne. Wish you were here."

"Oh well, we can open another bottle tomorrow when I give you my present. Have a great evening."

Then, as I put the phone down, I suddenly didn't want to wait until tomorrow. I wanted to be with her now.

I got in my car and drove fast. It took a couple of hours but I kept thinking how surprised Lady would be. I would give her the present. But that wasn't all. I had bought a ring and I was going to ask her to marry me.

It was almost dark when I got there but the air was still warm. Lights were on in the living room and the window was open. I could hear music – they were listening to 'Love is the Answer'. I looked through the window and saw them.

Marco and Lady were dancing. Arms round each other. Close. Very close.

As I watched them, Lady raised her face and Marco bent down and kissed her lips. Their mouths were open. Their bodies pressed together. Then Marco took Lady's hand and pulled her towards the stairs. A few moments later the light came on in Marco's bedroom.

I ran to the car and drove away. I drove for miles, hardly knowing where I was going. Then I stopped and rang Toddie.

"I've found her," I said. "I've found Lady."

"Where?"

"She's with Marco, Toddie. She left you for Marco."

Chapter 18

The Shooting

I won't pretend. No excuses. I knew exactly what I was doing when I rang Toddie. I knew exactly how he would react. I knew exactly what he would do.

I met him as he came off the motorway and I saw that crazy look burning in his eyes. He followed me to the house. We stopped our cars a little way down the road so that they wouldn't hear us coming.

I had the key of the house, but I didn't want Toddie to know that. I used my credit card to slip the latch of the front door. Quietly, we climbed the stairs. I pointed to Marco's room and Toddie opened the door. Moonlight was pouring through the window onto the bed.

Marco and Lady were curled up together. We stood for a long moment looking at them. They were like the Babes in the Wood. Beautiful. So much in love.

I hated them.

Toddie turned on the light and pulled back the bed-clothes. They were naked and as they woke up they tried to cover themselves.

"Get up!" Toddie ordered, pointing his gun at them.

They stood up, then grabbed their dressing gowns and put them on.

"Listen, Toddie …" Marco began.

"Shut up," Toddie ordered. "Downstairs, both of you."

Slowly, so slowly, they went down those stairs and into the living room. Toddie made them sit on the sofa. He sat in a chair and just stared at them.

"Toddie, please – we're family ..." Marco said, then stopped as Toddie raised the gun.

Long minutes of silence went by and I felt as if my heart would explode. I hated them both – Marco and Lady. I hated them, but I loved them. And I was killing them.

"It was you, Perry," Lady said. "You told him."

The look on her face filled me with shame. "Let her go," I said to Toddie. "Let Lady go."

"Shut up!" Toddie snapped. "She's mine. I decide what happens to her."

"No!" Lady shouted. "I am not yours. You do not own me."

Then slowly, oh so slowly, she reached out and took Marco's hand. She raised it to her lips and kissed it.

"Don't!" Toddie shouted.

But Lady kissed Marco's hand again. "I love him," she said. And smiled.

Then Toddie fired.

The first shot blew a hole in Marco's throat. The second shot hit him in the chest. He slumped to the side.

"Marco!" Lady screamed, putting her arms round him and pulling him up.

Marco groaned in agony and the sound came out from the hole in his throat. He coughed as his lungs filled up with blood. His legs twitched and kicked but Lady held onto him.

Marco gasped and struggled to take another breath. Blood bubbled from his throat then he stopped moving. But Lady still held onto him. She rocked him and ran her hands through his dark curls.

"He's dead," Toddie snarled. "He's dead, Lady. And now you belong to me."

"No, I do not," she said. "I belong to no-one." She bent and kissed Marco's face then she looked up at us, coldly. "I love him," Lady said. "I love him. And I spit on you. I spit on both of you."

Toddie raised his gun.

"No! Don't!" I yelled.

Toddie fired.

Lady jumped as if in shock, and then sat still. I thought he had missed. Then I saw the blood begin to stain her dressing gown. He had shot her through the heart.

Lady's eyes were wide and dead. And they seemed to be staring straight at me.

I ran out of the house, onto the lawn, and fell on my knees. I looked up at the black night sky. Millions of stars stared down at me, as cold as Lady's dead eyes. There was nowhere to hide

A shiver ran through me. I leaned forward and was sick. Sweat was running down my sides but I felt icy. I stood up and went back to the house.

Toddie was still there, sitting in the chair, looking at Marco and Lady. He glanced up at me as I went in. His eyes were as empty and dead as Lady's. He stood up. His gun fell to the floor. Slowly, almost as if he was drunk, he made his way towards the door.

I looked at Lady and a huge pain ripped through me. I picked up the gun. Toddie was at the door.

I wanted to shout but the word came out as a whisper – "Toddie!"

He heard me and turned. He looked at the gun then up at me.

He didn't say a word. But I swear to you, his eyes were telling me what to do. "Yes," his eyes seemed to say. "Please – do it. I've killed my family. Finish me now."

My finger slid onto the trigger.

Toddie smiled at me. He smiled at me and nodded. Then he started to move towards me.

I fired. He jerked backwards. I had hit his arm. Then he staggered towards me again.

"Do it! Do it!" his eyes said.

I fired again. And again.

The shots hit him in the chest and he fell back.

He took a long time to die. A long, terrible time. I sat on the floor and held him in my arms. He trembled with the pain.

"Oh God, Toddie, I'm sorry. I'm sorry," I said. "Please don't die. I'll get a doctor."

He shook his head and closed his eyes. He lay still for a long time and I thought he was dead. Then his mouth moved. He was trying to say something.

I bent my ear to his lips. The words came out softly like the wind through the trees.

"Wipe ... gun ... put it in ... Marco's hand ... Finger ... prints."

I squeezed his hand to show that I understood.

Then one more word came out, soft and gentle as a sigh.

"Friend."

His body grew heavy in my arms. He was dead.

Chapter 19

The Story

I drove back to my flat. I slept for a few hours then I got up and burned my bloody clothes, one by one.

On Saturday morning a postman went to the house. He saw the bodies through the window and called the police.

The police came to see me. They had found the gun in Marco's hand but Toddie's fingerprints were on it, too.

"We think one of the men killed the girl. Then they had a fight and killed each other," the detective told me. "But we can't work out why."

I don't know," I said. "I just work for Marco Investments. But ..."

"But what?"

"Well, I know Marco and Toddie had a couple of big rows lately."

"What about?"

"Well, I'm not sure but ... I think they were both mixed up with ... No, look, I can't ..."

"Come on," the detective said. "Mixed up with what?"

"I can't prove it but ... OK, I think they were mixed up with ... with selling drugs and

Marco wanted to set up on his own or something. But, listen, I'm not sure."

That's all it took. The police already knew about Toddie's drug dealing. But they'd never been able to pin anything on him. Now I was giving them proof. And they were happy to believe that Marco had been involved.

So, that became the story. And the newspaper headline was DRUG GANG KILLINGS.

Only I knew the truth – the truth about how we were all caught up, Toddie and Lady and Marco and me. We were caught up, all of us. Love is the answer.

Like the song says: *What makes life worth living? Love is, love is the answer.*

I killed love.

And life is not worth living.

Barrington Stoke would like to thank all its readers for commenting on the manuscript before publication and in particular:

Elizabeth Allen
Siobhan Arthur
Stacie Clark
Simon Collins
Frances Evitt
Simi Gill
Corey Gilmore
Trenicia Gould
Conor Grant
Jamie Hamilton
Anneka Jane Harper
Nicky Hitchcock

Rachel Hughes
Edward Hunter
Jamie-Lea Jennings
Ashleigh Law
Neil Malcolm
Shane Pakium
Jamie Shanley
Carrie Stormc .t
Patrick Tobin
Carol Watson
Alexandra L. Whitaker

Become a Consultant!

Would you like to give us feedback on our titles before they are published? Contact us at the email address below – we'd love to hear from you!

Email: info@barringtonstoke.co.uk
Website: www.barringtonstoke.co.uk